For Sadie

First published in 2003 by Macmillan Children's Books
A division of Macmillan Publishers Ltd
20 New Wharf Road, London N1 9RR
Basingstoke and Oxford
Associated companies worldwide
www.panmacmillan.com

Produced by Fernleigh Books
1A London Road, Enfield
Middlesex EN2 6BN

Text copyright © 2003 Fernleigh Books
Illustration copyright © 2003 Piers Harper

ISBN 1 405 03509 9 (HB)
ISBN 1 405 04773 9 (PB)

1 3 5 7 9 8 6 4 2 (HB)
1 3 5 7 9 8 6 4 2 (PB)

A CIP catalogue record for this book is available
from the British Library.

Manufactured in China.

LITTLE OWL

Illustrated by Piers Harper

MACMILLAN CHILDREN'S BOOKS

Little Owl lived in a nest in a tree at the edge of the wood. His brother and sister lived in the tree too, and Mummy Owl looked after them all.

Every night, Little Owl practised flapping his wings. One day soon, he would be able to fly on his own, but Mummy Owl said he had to be big and strong first.

"Look at me, Mummy!" said Little Owl, as he flapped his wings very fast. "I'm a big owl now, aren't I?"

"Yes, you're getting very big," said Mummy Owl, "but you're still not quite big enough to fly on your own. Not just yet."

Little Owl's wings drooped. "Will it be soon?" he asked.

"Very soon," said Mummy Owl. "Why don't we practise together now?"

"Hello Squirrel," said Little Owl. "Where have you been?"

"I've been exploring," said Squirrel, "all the way
up to the top of the tree!"
Little Owl bounced up and down on the branch.

"That sounds like a good place for flying!" he said.

"It's one of the *best* places for flying,"
said Mummy Owl. "Follow me
and I'll show you."

Up and up they flew, higher than Little Owl had ever
flown before. Then the two owls, one big and one small,
looked at the setting sun. It was *very* beautiful.
But Little Owl looked down and felt scared.
The top of the tree was very, very high.

"I think I'd like to go home now," he said.
"Of course we can," said Mummy Owl.
"You've been a very brave owl indeed."

Back at the nest, a family of rabbits were
playing beneath the old oak tree.

"Hello," said Little Owl. "Where have you been?"

"We've been playing in the meadow," said the biggest rabbit.
"It's a very good place for jumping."

Little Owl couldn't jump very well, but he thought
he might like to see the meadow. "Can we practise
flying there, too?" he asked Mummy Owl.

"Yes," she said. "Come on, Little Owl, follow me."

Little Owl watched the rabbits playing.
The meadow *was* a good place for jumping.
But Little Owl wasn't sure if it was a good place for flying.
It was too big and there were no trees. He thought about the safe,
wide branches of the big, old oak.

"Can we go home?" said Little Owl, flapping
his wings in a quiet kind of way.
Mummy Owl looked at her baby and saw that he was tired.
"Of course we can," she said.

On the way home, the two owls stopped for a rest.
A deer was nibbling the grass nearby.

"Hello," said Little Owl. "Where have you been?"

"I've been running beside the river," she said.
"It's the fastest thing in the whole forest!"

"Faster than you?" said Little Owl. "Then it must
be very fast indeed."

"And beautiful too," said Mummy Owl.
"Come, Little Owl, I'll show you."

At last, they came back to the safe, warm nest.
"Hello Bat," said Little Owl. "Did you see me flying?"
"Yes," said Bat, "you were very good! Why don't we go and play races?"
Now, Little Owl loved flying more than anything,
but he began to worry.

The river was very fast *and* very noisy. When they flew
close to the water, Little Owl decided that the
river wasn't a good place for flying either.
The water was just *too* fast – he couldn't keep up,
no matter how hard he flapped his wings.
"Shall we go home now?" he said.
"Of course," said Mummy Owl. "You've been very brave."
But as Little Owl followed her home,
he didn't feel like a very brave owl at all.

What if he felt scared?
There were lots of places that were too high
and too big and too fast for a little owl.
"But I can't go on my own," he said, "can I, Mummy?"
Mummy Owl looked at Little Owl. "I think that
you're quite strong enough, and brave enough,"
she said. "You're a big owl now."

Little Owl puffed out his chest and flapped
his wings as hard as he could. If Mummy
said he could do it, then it must be true!
Little Owl followed Bat through the trees,
up and down, and between all the branches.

"This is fun!" Little Owl thought.
After all, he wasn't really on his own,
not when Bat was there.

But Bat was much faster than Little Owl
and soon left him behind. Little Owl gasped.
He was all on his own! He began to feel
very frightened.

But then he remembered what Mummy Owl
had said. He was a big owl now. And that meant
he was strong and brave.
"I *can* fly on my own," he thought proudly.

Little Owl flew back to the nest.

"Look at me, Mummy!" he said. "I can fly all on my own!"

"Of course you can," said Mummy Owl. "I knew you could."

Then she folded Little Owl in her wings and hugged him tight.

"You're big and strong," she said, "and very, very brave."